KEYHOLDERS #3

INSIDE
THE
MAGIC

D1009220

STARSCAPE BOOKS BY
DEBBIE DADEY
AND MARCIA THORNTON JONES

s #3

INSIDE THE MAGIC

Debbie Dadey and Marcia Thornton Jones

Illustrated by Adam Stower

STARSCAPE

A TOM DOHERTY ASSOCIATES BOOK • NEW YORK

KEYHOLDERS #3: INSIDE THE MAGIC

Copyright © 2009 by Debra S. Dadey and
Marcia Thornton Jones

The Wrong Side of Magic excerpt copyright © 2009
by Debra S. Dadey and Marcia Thornton Jones

Illustrations and map copyright © 2009 by Adam Stower

A Starscape Book
Published by Tom Doherty Associates, LLC
175 Fifth Avenue
New York, NY 10010

www.tor-forge.com

ISBN 978-0-7653-5984-1

First Edition: November 2009

Printed in September 2009 in the United States of America by Offset
Paperback Manufacturers, Dallas, Pennsylvania

0 9 8 7 6 5 4 3 2 1

In memory of Ruth Dadey,
who brought magic to Meadowvale School
in Johnstown, Pennsylvania, for thirty-five years as
the volunteer "Bus Lady" and gave feisty its meaning.
She will be sorely missed by everyone who knew her.

And to Tom McMahon, thanks for being a true fan.
—DD

To Robert E. Thornton and Randall J. Thornton,
who led the way into the magic . . . I'll see you on the
other side!
—MTJ

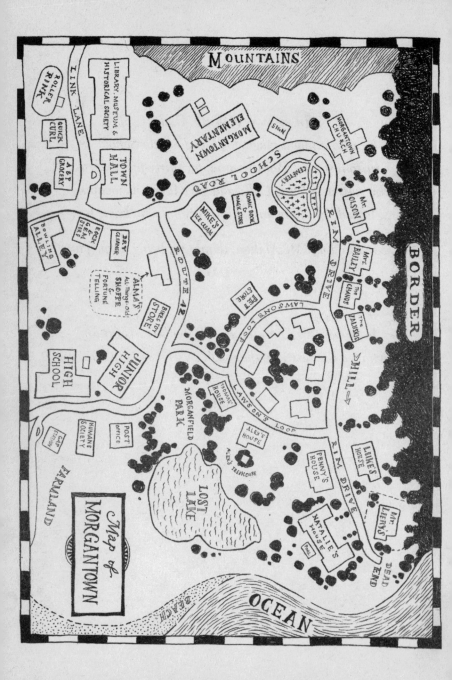

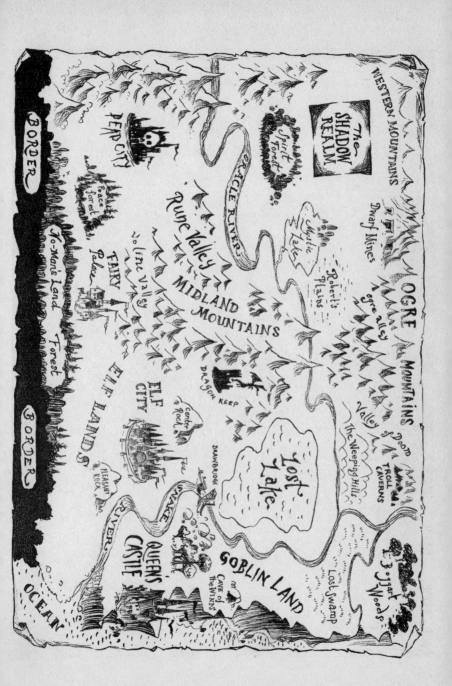

INSIDE THE MAGIC

1

"Is he dead?" Luke whispered.

Natalie pushed Luke aside. "Of course Mo isn't dead. See his sides moving? That means he's still breathing."

"But just barely," Penny said, falling to her knees beside Mo.

When Luke, Penny, and Natalie opened the door to Mr. Leery's house, they had expected to find Mo waiting impatiently. Instead they found a huge pile of feathers motionless on the floor.

Usually, their neighbor's link took the form of a big spotted cat. But when he discovered Mr. Leery had been kidnapped by the Queen of the Boggarts, Mo had turned into his natural form of a griffin.

"Be careful, Penny," Luke warned his best friend.

Penny smoothed the crest of feathers on Mo's head. He looked nothing like a cat anymore. For one thing, he was a lot bigger. Not only that, he had a wicked beak, talons, and powerful wings.

Just a few weeks earlier, Natalie, Luke, and Penny had been three normal kids living in Morgantown. In that short time they had found out that the thick tangle of hedges at the edge of their town was actually a border between the world they knew and a land of magic, and that they had been chosen by a wizard as apprentice Keyholders.

As Keyholders, the kids were chosen to maintain the border and keep the magic world from leaking into the real world. Part of being a Keyholder was wonderful; for example, having a link—an unbreakable lifelong bond with a magical creature. Mo had been Mr. Leery's link for nearly two hundred years. Kirin, a dazzling young unicorn, had selected Penny. Dracula, a rambunctious dragon about the size of a Doberman pinscher, picked Luke. Natalie, on the other hand, wasn't thrilled that she had been chosen by a rat named Buttercup.

Now Penny found herself cradling the head of a beast with talons that could rip a T. rex in half. It was a lot for a fifth grader to handle.

Mo closed his eyes as a spasm shot through his body. Blue, red, green, and orange feathers drifted to the floor. When he opened his eyes again, they were dull and cold. "The Boggart Queen cast a spell. A spell even more powerful than Leery," he whispered.

Humans and their links from the magical realm were so closely connected that when something happened to one, it affected the other. Judging from the way Mo was suffering, whatever had happened to Mr. Leery was bad. Very bad.

"This is your fault," Luke told Natalie. "If you hadn't taken so long packing your stupid pink suitcases we would've been here to help Mo."

"It is not my fault," Natalie said, glaring at Penny. "She wanted to pack, too."

Penny felt guilty. "Natalie's right," Penny said. "I took too long deciding what I needed in the magic land." She looked up at her link. Kirin had once used her unicorn horn to help Penny when she had been hurt rolling down a hill in a garbage can. "Can you help Mo?" she pleaded.

Kirin swished her tail back and forth. "Of course I can," she snapped.

"Wait!" Buttercup squealed, but Kirin kneeled before the fallen griffin and touched her horn to the place right above Mo's heart.

Mo shuddered as if cold water gushed through his veins. A green spark exploded from the spot where Kirin's horn touched the griffin's feathers.

"Ouch!" screamed the unicorn. She fell to the floor as if she'd been struck by lightning.

"What happened?" Penny shrieked.

Dracula bounced across Mr. Leery's living room. "Fire! Fire! Fire!" the small dragon

shrieked, sending little flames of his own shooting through the air.

"Stop it! Everyone!" shouted a little, yet very powerful voice. Buttercup was usually a meek rat, but she stomped a back paw in frustration. "The spell on Leery was powerfully cast with a protective shield. Not even unicorn magic can break it."

Kirin struggled up in a clatter of hooves. Her eyes crossed and she snorted when she saw her beautiful horn charred and covered with ash. "My horn! What has that evil queen done to my horn?"

"Your horn will heal itself," Buttercup said. "We have other things to worry about."

Kirin swished her tail so hard she slapped Natalie on the behind. "What is more important than my horn?" the unicorn snapped.

"Leery is," Buttercup pointed out. "And Mo."

Mo lifted his head and whimpered. He had to force out every word. "Find Bridger. He will know. He can help."

The kids stared in horror when Mo's bones

popped and cracked. His body turned in on itself as black hair pushed the feathers from his skin. His beak curled inward until it became the face of a cat. In less than a minute, the griffin was gone and a black spotted cat with curled ears lay before them.

"Mo?" Penny asked. "Can you hear us?"

"He *has* to be able to hear us," Luke said. "We can't find Leery without his help."

But Mo didn't answer them. His breathing was shallow and his paws twitched as if he were locked inside a very bad dream.

"We should call the police," Penny said.

"No!" Kirin told her. "No one can know about the Shadow Realm. No one."

"Besides," Buttercup added, "the police would never believe you."

"Maybe a doctor can help Mo," Luke suggested.

Dracula nudged Luke. "No doctor knows boggart spells."

"The Boggart Queen must be stopped," Natalie said. "And I'm just the one to do it."

"A-hem," came a little voice from the floor.

Natalie looked at her link. "With Buttercup's help, of course."

Dracula hopped up and down. "Stop the Queen! Stop her! Stop her!"

Penny clenched her jaw. Before being kidnapped, Mr. Leery had been training them to find and fix leaks in the border. Natalie was a natural at it. Not Penny and Luke. It rubbed Penny's nerves raw that Natalie could do something better than she could.

"Stop bragging," Luke told Natalie. "Just because you're better at finding leaks in the border, it doesn't mean you're ready to fight the Boggart Queen."

Natalie tapped Luke on the nose with a finger. "I'm more ready than you are."

"Stop it!" Penny said, shoving Natalie and Luke apart. "We need to take care of Mo. Then we'll figure out what to do next."

Luke nodded. "I'll get a pillow and blanket."

"Fine," Natalie said. "I'll get some water."

Kirin blew warm air over the cat, but she was careful not to touch his body. Dracula cried a purple tear when Penny and Luke gently placed Mo on a pillow and covered him up to his chin with a blanket. The cat's whiskers twitched and Mo groaned.

"Where is Natalie with that water?" Penny asked.

"I'll check," Luke said.

After a few minutes, Luke came back to the room waving a piece of paper in the air. "She's gone," he said. "All she left was this note."

Penny looked at Natalie's scrawled words. "'Gone to save the world!'" Penny read out loud. "Is she nuts? We have to catch up to her! She can't do it alone."

"We should let her try," Luke said. "It would serve her right to fail."

Penny grabbed Luke's arm. "But if she fails, she could die. We can't let that happen. Even if it is Natalie."

Luke sighed. "You're right. We'd better hurry."

Luke glanced around the room once more before leaving. He noticed Mr. Leery's walking stick propped in the corner. Luke reached for it, the carved wood feeling solid and fitting his palm perfectly.

"Why are you taking that?" Penny asked.

Luke gripped the stick firmly in his hand. "Because," he said, "I have a feeling Mr. Leery will need it on the way back."

"If we make it that far," Penny said.

2

"How did Natalie get through?" Penny asked as they stood looking at the thick wall of trees, bushes, and vines behind Mr. Leery's house. Penny knew the answer to her own question. Natalie was much more talented as a Keyholder. She had already mastered how to repair leaks in the border. Penny hadn't even been able to sense where the openings were.

Kirin nudged Penny toward the border. "You're a Keyholder. Why don't you act like one?"

Dracula hopped up and down. "Let me try. Let me try."

Luke placed his hand on his link's head to

stop him from bouncing. "Maybe if we try together," he said.

Dracula snuggled beside him and they closed their eyes. Luke's forehead wrinkled as he focused. Minutes passed and nothing happened. Penny was ready to give up hope when she heard a pop.

"You did it!" she shouted, but then there was silence and Luke fell to the ground.

"It's no use," Luke said. "I tried as hard as I could and all I got was a little snap. My cereal makes more noise than that."

Penny felt like crying, but then Kirin nuzzled her arm and whispered, "Help him."

"I can't . . ."

Luke grabbed Penny's arm. "Mr. Leery chose us for a reason. You have to try."

"But I'm not ready," Penny said. "I haven't practiced enough."

Luke knew that Penny always studied for weeks for a test, but he also knew that they were out of time. "This is a pop quiz that we can't fail."

Penny nodded and stood next to Luke. Together, the two Keyholders faced the border. Their links stood behind them, gently nuzzling their shoulders. They stood for a long time. Never in all his years of playing basketball had Luke struggled this hard. Never in all her studying, had Penny focused so intensely.

If their eyes had been open, they would have noticed a small wave in the air from their hands to the border. The wave turned into a ripple. Finally, the bushes clicked, clacked, and split open, creating a path for the kids and their links.

"You did it! You did it!" Dracula cheered.

Luke and Penny opened their eyes. "We did?"

"Don't stand around admiring your efforts," Kirin said. "Go before it closes."

"Go! Go! Go!" Dracula shouted, a small puff of smoke forming around his nose with each word.

Luke took a deep breath and led the way into the magic world. As soon as the group was through, the bushes clicked and clacked back together. In a few seconds, there was no indication there had ever been an opening.

None of them moved when they saw one of Natalie's pink rolling suitcases abandoned in a tall clump of thorny weeds. The zipper had been torn away. Clothes were strewn across their path and pink hair ribbons, socks, and underwear hung from tree branches.

"Oh, no," Penny whispered. "We're too late. Something horrible must have happened to her."

"Bad. Bad," Dracula mumbled. A tendril of nervous smoke floated from his nostrils.

A tunnel of trees, bushes, and vines led them deeper into the magic land. The sound of scurrying from both sides of the passageway made the kids turn in a circle.

"Bridger?" Penny said hopefully. "Is that you?"

Bridger was the Lead Elf of Pleasant Rock and one of Mr. Leery's friends. He was also the only one Mo said could help them. On the few times the kids had passed through the border with Mr. Leery, Bridger had always been waiting for them.

"Maybe we should go back," Luke said as something slithered in the bushes near him.

A scream stopped him. "Help me! Somebody help me!"

It sounded just like Natalie. Penny and Luke didn't think twice. They took off down the path with Kirin and Dracula close on their heels.

They hurdled another one of Natalie's suitcases and dodged piles of designer clothes until they reached a small clearing. A screech brought them to a stop. Luke looked up into the treetops to see a skinny goblin dangling Natalie by her feet. Two more goblins giggled in nearby trees. One of them wore Natalie's nightgown.

"It's a trap!" Penny gasped.

"And Natalie led us right into it," Luke added.

Natalie's hair hung down in long strands. Goblin goop dripped from the ends and plopped on the ground. Buttercup dangled out of Natalie's pocket, whiskers and tail trembling.

"We got them! We got them!" chanted the goblins. The one wearing Natalie's nightgown scratched his butt as it swung from tree to tree in a dizzying dance of arms and legs.

Goblin slime splattered all around Penny and Luke. They had to hop away to keep from getting drenched.

"Do something!" Natalie screamed. "They're planning to take us to the Queen!"

"What can we do?" Luke yelled. "It's hopeless."

Penny reached down and grabbed a handful of rocks. She shoved them into Luke's hand. "As long as we have breath, we have hope. You do your thing and I'll do mine!"

It was a known fact that Luke had the best aim of all the basketball players in Morgantown, and Penny was the fastest runner in their school. She proved it right then. She scattered leaves and dirt as she darted first one way, then another.

"Get her! Get her!" screeched the night-

gown goblin. Just then Luke hurled a rock. It hit the goblin right on the forehead. *"Aaaacck!"* screeched the goblin as it tumbled from a branch and crashed to the ground.

The goblin chasing Penny tried to keep up. When Penny zigged, the goblin zigged. When Penny zagged, the goblin zagged. Unfortunately for the goblin, it had to keep its eyes on Penny. That's why it didn't see the giant tree until it was too late.

Thunk! The goblin ran smack-dab into the trunk and slid down to the ground.

Dracula inhaled turkberries from a nearby bush. Dracula loved turkberries, but was allergic to them. Usually, a sneezing dragon is a problem. Not this time. He sniffed. He snorted. Then he let out a sneeze so powerful that a flame shot straight up the tree to the goblin holding Natalie's sneakers.

"Aaaaaahhhhhhh!" screamed Natalie as the goblin dropped her.

"Aaaaaahhhhhhh!" screamed Buttercup from Natalie's pocket as they both fell like rotten apples.

Kirin galloped under Natalie just in time. "Hang on," Kirin warned before she leaped out of the way of the falling goblin.

One goblin swatted his smoking behind. Another rubbed a knot on his head. The third was crying over his skinned knees and elbows. All three glared at the Keyholders and their links.

"Uh-oh," Natalie said as she scrambled off Kirin and grabbed her backpack from the ground. "They don't look very happy."

"I think we better get out of here," Penny said. "Fast."

"We're right behind you," Luke said. "*Run!*"

3

Kirin crashed through thick underbrush.
Dracula dodged limbs and branches. Penny,
Luke, and Natalie hurtled through the woods
after the two links. Buttercup clung to Natalie's pocket.

"Stop!" Natalie finally gasped. "I. Can't.
Breathe."

Luke and Penny slowed to a stop. All three
kids bent over, grabbing their sides and gulping air.

Dracula circled overhead, searching the
forest for goblins. "I think we've lost them,"
he told Luke.

Kirin shook her head, sending leaves flying

from her mane. "But not for long," she warned. "We aren't safe anywhere on this side of the border."

"I hate goblins," Natalie complained. "Why am I always the one getting slimed?" She shook her head and slung goblin slime into nearby bushes. Wherever slime landed, the bushes cringed and the leaves curled up.

"Slime! Slime!" Dracula said, landing beside them and bouncing with each word.

"Can't you use that horn of yours to clean us up?" Natalie asked Kirin.

The unicorn looked at her as if she had just suggested they eat slugs for breakfast. "My horn is not a washrag," she snorted.

"Then what good is it?" Natalie blurted.

"Leave Kirin out of this," Penny told Natalie. "This is your fault."

"Mine?" Natalie snapped right back. "I didn't do anything."

"Yes, you did," Luke said. "You sneaked out of Leery's without waiting for us."

Buttercup crawled out of Natalie's pocket.

"Excuse me," she said, but the kids were so busy complaining they didn't hear.

Buttercup tugged on Natalie's sleeve. "Excuse me," she said again.

"Not now, Buttercup," Natalie said, putting the rat down on a pile of dried leaves.

"You should be nicer to your link," Penny said. "At least she's not mad at you like we are. You nearly got us captured by goblins."

"I told you, it isn't my fault," Natalie argued. "How was I supposed to know they'd be waiting for me as soon as I slipped through the border? If you ask me, it's that little squirt, Bridger's, fault. He should've been here. Isn't he supposed to always be at our beck and call?"

"Don't let Bridger hear you calling him a squirt," Penny said.

"Elves serve no one," Kirin added. "*You'd better* learn that lesson very fast."

"Fast! Fast! Fast!" repeated Dracula.

"Whatever," Natalie said. "We still need to find him."

"Natalie has a point," Luke said. "Bridger has always been here before. Where is he now?"

The kids looked around the woods. It was quiet. Too quiet. No chirping birds. No buzzing bees. Nothing.

"Where is everyone?" Penny whispered.

"That's what I've been trying to tell you," Buttercup said from her spot near Natalie's sneakers. A back paw thumped impatiently. "They're not here. But I know the way to their village. Follow me quickly." Buttercup scurried down the trail.

"Wait!" Natalie said. "I have to go back and repack my suitcases."

"No time," Buttercup called over her shoulder. "There's no time. You'll just have to make do with what's in your backpack."

"Oh, rats," Natalie huffed and snatched her backpack off the ground. Then she looked to make sure Buttercup hadn't heard.

Luke and Penny hurried after Buttercup. Dracula zipped along overhead, his wings slashing at trees and causing leaves to rain down on them. Kirin snorted when leaves landed on her back.

Natalie's arms were crossed and she stomped extra hard as she brought up the

{23}

rear. "This," she grumbled, "is not my idea of a good time. I can't believe my hair is slimed again *and* my things are probably ruined. My father paid a fortune for those clothes."

They walked for a long time in the shade of the tall timbers with Natalie grumbling the whole way. Finally, Buttercup paused beside an enormous silver rock. Natalie touched one of the hundreds of diamonds glistening in the boulder. The effect was like looking at thousands of tiny rainbows. "Oh, look how they sparkle," Natalie said. "I must have one."

"Stop her!" Buttercup screeched.

Whomp! Dracula hit her from behind.

Thump! Kirin pushed Natalie so hard she fell to her knees.

"Hey! Why'd you do that?" Natalie yelled.

"Those are mesmerizing stones," Buttercup told her. "If you look directly into one for more than thirteen seconds you become entranced until Bridger decides to break the spell. It's one of the magics the elves use to protect their village."

"Then we're almost there?" Penny asked.

"It's a good thing," Luke said. "The more time it takes us, the more danger for Mr. Leery."

"And Mo," added Kirin.

Penny twined her fingers in Kirin's mane and rested her forehead on Kirin's neck. "We'll never forget about Mo," Penny assured her link.

"Bridger will know what to do," Luke said, trying to reassure everyone, including himself. "He'll make everything okay."

"Well, I wish he'd hurry up and get here," Natalie said, wiping dirt from her knees.

"Me, too," Penny said.

"Where is he?" Luke asked.

Buttercup's ears twitched and she pulled on her whiskers. "He should be here," she said. "It's not like the elves to allow strangers to march into the village. Where are the sentries? Where are the archers?"

"Sentries?" Penny asked.

"Archers?" Luke asked.

"Of course," Buttercup said. "You didn't

expect the most powerful elf in the Shadow Realm not to have protection, did you?"

The three kids looked around, searching for archers with arrows pointing at their hearts.

"Don't bother," Kirin said. "If an elf doesn't want to be seen, he won't be."

"Besides," Buttercup said, "there are no elves here."

"What do you mean, there are no elves?" Natalie said. "You said you knew the way to the elves' camp."

"And I do," Buttercup told her link. "The camp is straight ahead, but I don't feel the presence of elves."

"Well, come on," Natalie said. "Let's go find them."

Natalie stomped past Buttercup and led the way down the trail. Buttercup scampered through the leaves, close on Natalie's heels. Penny and Luke hurried after them. The path narrowed until Natalie had to push through an opening in the trees that formed a circle around a clearing.

"We're here," Buttercup said.

A thick canopy of branches concealed most of the tops of the trees, but Penny got a peek at several cottages nestled amongst high limbs. They looked like colorful dollhouses, complete with shutters and miniature smokestacks. But today, no smoke rose from the chimneys.

Dracula hiccupped and Kirin's tail flicked with unease. "Where is everyone?" Penny whispered.

Twang!

Twang!

Twang!

Three arrows whooshed through the branches, sticking upright in the dirt just in front of the kids' toes.

4

Three elves jumped from the trees and landed in front of Natalie. "We're under attack!" Natalie screamed. "This is the worst day ever!"

"We are not under attack," Buttercup said. "If they had wanted to kill us, we would already be dead. They were just welcoming us."

Natalie pushed a slime-covered piece of hair off her face. "Well, that's a fine way to say hello. Do they poke you with swords to say good-bye?"

"Don't tempt them," Kirin warned.

Three short and rather plump elves wearing clothes made from tree bark and carrying bows stood before them. Quivers of arrows hung on their shoulders and their belts held knives of varying sizes. The elves were small, but tough. Very tough. The female elf spoke, but the words sounded like they were getting caught in her throat.

"What is she saying?" Penny whispered.

"It's Elfin," Kirin explained. "I don't speak it."

A male elf with a scar that ran from his ear to his chin stepped forward. His words were heavily accented, but the kids were able to understand them.

"We are scouts, sent by his most royal self, Bridger of Pleasant Rock."

"Thank goodness," Penny said. "We need Bridger's help. Can we see him?"

"I am sorry," the elf told them. "Bridger is gone."

"Gone?" Natalie blurted. "But we need him! Something happened to Mr. Leery."

"Mo, too! Mo, too," Dracula added.

"We have to save them both," Penny said. "Bridger is our only hope."

"Can you take us to Bridger?" Luke asked. "Mo said Bridger could help us find Mr. Leery."

"Bridger has taken our villagers to a secure location far away from the Queen and her magic. Too much time would lapse if we led you to him. Bridger instructed us to await your arrival and assist you in freeing Leery. He leaves it up to you to save him. To save us all."

"See?" Natalie told Penny and Luke. "I told you I could do this. We don't need Bridger."

"But we don't know anything about battling an evil queen," Penny reminded Natalie.

The three elves bowed. "We will accompany you."

"Let's get a move on," Natalie said. "Which way do we go?"

The three elves erupted into chatter. One pointed east. Another pointed north. The third pointed west.

"Great," Natalie said. "We're being led into the Shadow Realm by the Three Stooges."

The one elf that spoke English glared at her. "The Realm is a land of many options. It is our desire to choose the safest."

Luke shook his head. "Safe is good, but fast is better."

The elves looked at each other as if they were passing secret messages between them. The female elf gave a tiny nod, finally making the decision, and the elf with the scar began to speak.

"Our spies within the Shadow Realm confirm that the Queen's henchmen took him deep within her territory."

Buttercup squeaked. "Anywhere but there!"

"It is like a dagger in my heart to tell you it is true," the elf said. "We must cross the Snake River and head into the Goblin Lands— straight into the heart of the Queen's domain. Even then, we do not know exactly where he is being held. Our only hope is that one of our spies will locate the most high Leery and find us in time to guide us on our path."

"Snake River?" Natalie said. "That's just a name, right? It's not really full of snakes, is it?" Natalie even hated looking at a picture of a snake. The idea of a river full of them made her feel cold and clammy.

The elf looked at her for a full ten seconds.

"No need to worry about snakes until we get past the troll."

"Troll?" Luke asked.

"Of course," the elf told him. "But first, we must go north past Center Rock to Lost Lake. Once there, we'll veer east to reach the river. You must beware. The evil queen sent henchmen through the Realm, infiltrating our lands and setting magic traps. It is most lucky that you made it this far without being captured."

"Hello?" Natalie said, pointing to the goblin goop stuck in her hair. "Where do you think this came from!"

The elf bowed. "We are most glad you were able to escape. Let us hope goblin spit is the worst we encounter."

As they turned to lead the way down the trail, Penny saw the grim look the elves gave to each other. If she didn't know better, she would've said it was a look of complete hopelessness.

"Without Bridger, how will we know what to do?" Penny whispered to Luke.

"The scouts will help us," Luke said.

The three Keyholders and their links silently followed the scouts, noticing that they led the way with caution. Their eyes constantly roved: left, right, up, down.

Maybe if a cloud hadn't cast a shadow over them.

Maybe if Dracula hadn't sneezed and set fire to a bush.

Maybe if the scouts hadn't looked back to check for flames.

But a cloud did cast a shadow just as Dracula sneezed and the three scouts glanced back.

And it all happened at just the wrong time.

One, two, three. Each elf stepped into a circle of mushrooms growing on the forest floor. It was a small circle. A circle made just big enough for three.

The earth creaked and cracked. "NOOOOOO!" the lead elf cried, but then his voice shattered as if his vocal cords had turned to glass.

"Help them," Penny cried and rushed for-

ward. She would've dived right into the circle if Kirin hadn't knocked her down.

"Don't step inside the circle," Kirin said. "It's a trap."

Buttercup scurried around the circle one way, turned, then came back. "Kirin is right. Oh, dear me. This is bad, very bad."

"What is it?" Luke asked. He tried to be calm, but his voice was at least an octave higher than normal.

Buttercup grabbed one of Natalie's shoelaces and gnawed through the plastic end. "Tell us," Natalie said, pulling her foot out of reach.

"It's a powerful spell. A rooting spell," Buttercup told her. "There is nothing we can do to help them."

"No offense," Luke said, "but you're only a tiny rat. What do you know about boggart spells?"

Kirin snorted and Dracula jumped up and down. "Tell them. Tell them," Dracula said.

Buttercup shook her head. "Trust me, I

know about rooting spells. These elfin scouts will be forever rooted to the ground like tree stumps. Only Leery or Bridger can help them now."

"So to save them we must rescue Mr. Leery. But to rescue Mr. Leery we need the elves to show us the way," Luke reasoned, his voice going up another octave.

Penny faced her link. "You're from this side of the border. Don't you know the way to where that awful queen lives?"

Kirin dipped her head low until her horn rested on the ground. "I am sorry. But Dracula and I are still young. We've heard of many parts of the Shadow Realm, but we haven't been everywhere. Especially not to the Queen's region."

Dracula stopped fluttering and landed on Kirin's back. "Why would we? We never wanted to go *there*!"

"Then we've failed," Penny said. "We don't know the way."

"Not so fast," Natalie said. "I haven't failed at anything."

"Oh, please," Luke told her. "This is no time for bragging about how much better you are than us."

Natalie shook her head. "For your information, I was not bragging. I was just going to mention that the elves told us exactly where we have to go. East past Center Rock to Lost Lake then north to Snake River. Once we cross Snake River we'll be in the Goblin Lands where the Queen is keeping Mr. Leery. Remember?"

"She's right," Kirin said, lifting her head and looking at Penny hopefully. "We can at least get that far."

"But then what?" Penny asked.

"We'll think of something," Buttercup said from Natalie's shoe. "We have to."

"Do you really think we can do this alone?" Penny asked.

"We're not alone," Luke reminded her. "We have each other."

5

"Where are you going?" Luke asked his friends.

"This way," Natalie said, pointing off to the side.

"But here's a trail," Luke said, looking around the stone-like elves.

Natalie squinted until she made out the narrow path leading through a thick growth of bushes. "That's just an animal trail. This is the way we should go." She nodded at a wide path cut through the woods on their right. "It's the only way that goes to the east. Don't you remember, the elves said to go east?"

Penny looked at Natalie's path. It even had

an old wooden sign that said EAST in strange flowery letters. Then Penny looked at Luke's trail. "Natalie is right," Penny said. "That path is bigger."

"Of course, I'm right," Natalie said. "I'm always right." She began marching down the trail, not even checking to see if her fellow Keyholders and their links followed.

The trail was wide, level, and grassy. The ground was soft beneath their shoes and the trees kept them shaded. "This does seem like an easier trail," Luke said to Penny.

"Very easy," Penny said.

"Too easy," muttered Kirin.

"Wait!" Penny said, stopping in her tracks. "Didn't the elves say to go north first? To Lost Lake? We haven't seen a lake yet and the elves were taking us north."

"Oops. Wrong way. Wrong way!" Dracula swooped in front of them to block their path.

"Get out of my way, you silly dragon," Natalie snapped and walked around him. "I know what I'm doing."

She took two more steps.

Crack!

The ground broke beneath her sneaker.

"AHHHHHH!" Natalie screamed.

Whoosh!

Dracula swooped down and clutched Natalie's ponytail with his talons just as she fell into a deep hole. Dracula slung her back up onto the ground, then flopped down beside her, flinging tufts of blond hair from his talons.

Natalie scooted back from the hole screaming, "A trap! A trap! I could have died down there!"

Penny and Luke peered over the edge of the huge hole Natalie had fallen into. The kids couldn't even see the bottom it was so deep.

"If Dracula hadn't acted so fast, we'd all be at the bottom of that hole," Luke said.

Penny nodded. "Someone covered the trap with branches so we wouldn't see it until it was too late."

"I think we should take the other trail," Natalie said. She patted Dracula softly on the neck. "Thank you, Dracula. You saved my life."

The kids backtracked to where they had left the elves. They carefully made their way around the circle of mushrooms and the frozen elves.

"Don't worry," Luke told them. "We'll be back for you." His hand firmly gripped Mr. Leery's walking stick as he led the way into the unknown.

The kids walked for a long time without saying a word, lost in their own thoughts. Vines snagged their shirts and branches scratched at their arms. Bugs swarmed around their faces. The sun was starting to dip in the sky when Natalie couldn't take it anymore. "My feet are killing me," she complained. "I have to rest."

Penny nodded and pulled a canteen out of her backpack. "I need a drink."

Natalie was beside her in an instant. "Can I have some of that? Got anything to eat in that backpack? I'm hungry."

"Didn't you bring something to drink and eat?" Penny asked.

Natalie shook her head. It was still stringy

with goblin goo. "No, but if you want to listen to some music, I've got you covered." Natalie dumped two MP3 players, a handheld video game, mini speakers, and a brand new cell phone out of her backpack.

"Why in the world did you bring that stuff?" Luke asked.

Natalie rolled her eyes. "To keep from getting bored, of course," she said.

Penny handed her canteen to Natalie. "You should've worried about getting hungry instead. Do you want some cheese crackers?" Penny asked Luke.

Splash! Natalie dumped the entire contents of the canteen on her head.

"Stop!" Penny screamed. "We need that water to drink."

"I had to wash my hair," Natalie argued. "Don't worry, we can get some more. I'm sure there's a water fountain somewhere."

Luke would have laughed if he hadn't been so mad. "Are you crazy? We're in the middle of a magical wilderness. There are no water fountains!"

"Oops," Natalie said, water dripping off her hair.

Luke held up his water bottle. It was still mostly full. "Well, at least we have this bottle."

Plop! Luke's water bottle fell to the ground as a big hand scooped him up. "Spies," growled a huge, hideously ugly creature. "Evil goblin spies."

"Troll! Troll!" Dracula screamed.

Kirin instinctively stepped in front of Penny.

The troll was half as tall as a tree and his skin was as rough as bark. He looked so much like a tree that the kids hadn't noticed him standing there.

"Put me down," Luke said in the toughest-sounding voice he could muster. Of course, that was difficult since the troll was squeezing him a little too tightly for comfort.

"Down! Down!" Dracula yelled. "Or I'll huff and puff!"

Penny raced around Kirin and kicked the troll's big toe.

"*Urrrrgh!*" groaned the troll. He reached

Dracula squeezed close. "No can help," said the troll.

"But, I have strawberries," Penny said, quickly pulling a plastic bag filled with the red ripe fruit out of her backpack.

The troll smacked his lips. "Louis like strawberries."

Penny put the bag into the troll's huge hand. In an instant, Louis ate the strawberries, bag and all. He patted his tummy and closed his eyes. "Yum."

"Now, you have to help us find Mr. Leery," Penny said.

"Can't," said the troll, not even bothering to open his eyes.

"But we gave you our food," Penny said. "That means you owe us a favor."

Louis' eyes snapped open and he sighed. "Follow Louis." The ground shook with every step he took. Penny, Luke, Natalie, and their links raced after him.

The troll didn't stop until he came to a strip of land between a peaceful dark lake and a wide, roaring river. A wooden draw-

down to rub his toe, then snatched Penny and brought her up to his giant nose and gave a sniff. Penny saw the inside of the troll's nose and ducked to avoid a big booger.

"No smell like goblins," the troll said.

The troll licked Luke's cheek. "No taste like goblins."

Luke almost fainted from the bad breath.

"All right," Natalie screamed up at the troll. "I've had just about enough of this stupid magic land."

"Oh, dear," Buttercup said from Natalie's shoulder. The rat chewed on the end of Natalie's hair. "This is not the time to make him mad. Trolls live under the rule of the Boggart Queen."

Buttercup thought she was squeaking just loud enough for Natalie to hear, but the troll bent down.

"Not *me*!" he growled. "Not Louis! Louis not like Queen. Not like Goblin Land. Me stay *alone* on *this* side of the river!"

"You ran away from the Queen?" Kirin asked.

The troll sniffed. Giant tears pooled in his eyes. "Louis likes picking flowers. Not boogers. Other trolls laugh. Mean trolls. Who needs them?"

Penny patted the troll on his hand. "No one likes to be laughed at."

"We come in peace," Natalie added. "We're looking for Mr. Leery."

"Leery?" the giant said in a suddenly gentle voice. "Leery good. Bring me strawberries."

"I like strawberries, too," Penny said. "When did you last see Mr. Leery?"

Luke gasped as his hair was blown back by the troll's horrible breath. "Leery gone," growled Louis. "Hobbly-goblins stole nic Leery. Hobbly-goblins took nice Leery to me old Queen."

"You *saw* Mr. Leery?" Natalie yelled beside the troll's kneecap. "Can you t where they took him?"

The troll nodded. "Across river."

"Will you lead us there?" Natalie a

Louis shook his head and put Pe Luke on the ground. Immediately

down to rub his toe, then snatched Penny and brought her up to his giant nose and gave a sniff. Penny saw the inside of the troll's nose and ducked to avoid a big booger.

"No smell like goblins," the troll said.

The troll licked Luke's cheek. "No taste like goblins."

Luke almost fainted from the bad breath.

"All right," Natalie screamed up at the troll. "I've had just about enough of this stupid magic land."

"Oh, dear," Buttercup said from Natalie's shoulder. The rat chewed on the end of Natalie's hair. "This is not the time to make him mad. Trolls live under the rule of the Boggart Queen."

Buttercup thought she was squeaking just loud enough for Natalie to hear, but the troll bent down.

"Not *me*!" he growled. "Not Louis! Louis not like Queen. Not like Goblin Land. Me stay *alone* on *this* side of the river!"

"You ran away from the Queen?" Kirin asked.

The troll sniffed. Giant tears pooled in his eyes. "Louis likes picking flowers. Not boogers. Other trolls laugh. Mean trolls. Who needs them?"

Penny patted the troll on his hand. "No one likes to be laughed at."

"We come in peace," Natalie added. "We're looking for Mr. Leery."

"Leery?" the giant said in a suddenly gentle voice. "Leery good. Bring me strawberries."

"I like strawberries, too," Penny said. "When did you last see Mr. Leery?"

Luke gasped as his hair was blown back by the troll's horrible breath. "Leery gone," growled Louis. "Hobbly-goblins stole nice Leery. Hobbly-goblins took nice Leery to mean old Queen."

"You *saw* Mr. Leery?" Natalie yelled from beside the troll's kneecap. "Can you tell us where they took him?"

The troll nodded. "Across river."

"Will you lead us there?" Natalie asked.

Louis shook his head and put Penny and Luke on the ground. Immediately Kirin and

Dracula squeezed close. "No can help," said the troll.

"But, I have strawberries," Penny said, quickly pulling a plastic bag filled with the red ripe fruit out of her backpack.

The troll smacked his lips. "Louis like strawberries."

Penny put the bag into the troll's huge hand. In an instant, Louis ate the strawberries, bag and all. He patted his tummy and closed his eyes. "Yum."

"Now, you have to help us find Mr. Leery," Penny said.

"Can't," said the troll, not even bothering to open his eyes.

"But we gave you our food," Penny said. "That means you owe us a favor."

Louis' eyes snapped open and he sighed. "Follow Louis." The ground shook with every step he took. Penny, Luke, Natalie, and their links raced after him.

The troll didn't stop until he came to a strip of land between a peaceful dark lake and a wide, roaring river. A wooden drawbridge stood suspended in the air, half on each side of the river. "Can't help," Louis said again. "Hobbly-goblins break bridge."

"But we have to get across to save Mr. Leery," Luke said.

"Can't," Louis said again. "Bridge broke."

"Then all this has been for nothing," Natalie moaned. "The goblin goo. All the walking. Almost getting killed. My designer clothes ruined. All for nothing."

"Wait!" Buttercup said. "How do you make the bridge go down?"

Louis pointed to a lever. "Push. Go down. Mean hobbly-goblins smash. Don't work now."

"But if there's a lever here, wouldn't there also be a lever on the other side?" Luke asked.

Everyone looked across to the other half of the bridge. Sure enough, there was a lever.

"They didn't break that one," Penny said.

"No," Luke told her. "They would want to make sure they could lower the bridge from their side in case they want to come back over the river."

"Well, just swim over there and push it," Natalie said impatiently. "We're in a hurry."

"No swim." Louis pointed to the water. For the first time the kids noticed huge black snakes swirling in the river. Occasionally one jumped up out of the water and snapped at the air.

"Oh, that's just gross," Natalie said. "What is wrong with this place? Don't they have 1-800-Kll-Pest?"

Dracula hopped up and down. "I go. I go."

"That's a great idea," Penny said. "You can fly over there. All you have to do is land on the lever. That should be enough to lower the bridge."

"Be careful," Luke said. "Those snakes are jumping awfully high."

"Careful. Careful," Dracula repeated. Then with a big hop, he soared into the air. He flew high over the snapping snakes. Unfortunately, it wasn't high enough.

"Look out!" Luke shouted as an enormous night-colored serpent reared out of the water and clamped his fangs on Dracula's left wing.

The kids watched in horror as Dracula struggled to get away. "It's going to pull him under the water!" Penny shouted.

"*Nooooooo!*" Luke yelled, grabbing some rocks off the ground and chucking them at the huge snake. Most of the rocks fell into the water, but one caught the serpent right on his head. It let go of Dracula just long enough for him to flop onto a big boulder on the other side of the river. He lay there, very still.

"He's trapped over there, he's hurt, and we can't get to him," Penny said.

"Oh, yes we can," Luke said. He grabbed five fist-sized rocks. *Whiz*. The first one tapped the lever, but the bridge didn't budge.

"You've got to hit it harder," Natalie told him.

Luke bit his lip and threw the next rock with all his might.

Wham! The rock hit the lever and with a loud groan the bridge began to lower. "Now you can lead the way," Natalie told the troll.

The troll shook his head. "Never cross river. Louis stay here. Pick flowers. Not boogers."

"But we don't know the way to where the Queen lives, and you do," Natalie said.

The troll scratched his chin. Then he reached inside his dirty bark coat and pulled out a dirt-encrusted, rolled-up parchment. "Mother gave me. You take," Louis said.

Natalie squealed and held her nose, but Penny gratefully took the paper. "Is it a map of the Shadow Realm?" Kirin asked, looking over Penny's shoulder.

Louis nodded. "One true map."

Natalie rolled her eyes. "You have to be kidding. I bet there are tons of maps all over the place."

Louis sighed, "Beware other maps. Queen tricks. Directions bad." Louis used a dirty fingernail to gently tap the paper in Penny's hands. "One TRUE map."

"Thanks, Louis," Penny said. "We owe you our lives."

Luke nodded, but as soon as the bridge was almost all the way down, he raced across to check on Dracula.

"Can you help Dracula?" Penny asked Kirin.

"Of course I'll help the little turkberry-breath," Kirin said.

They hurried over the bridge, leaving Louis behind.

"I'm here, Dracula!" Luke shouted. He fell to his knees beside the fallen dragon. "I'm here. Wake up! *Please.*"

Kirin looked cross-eyed at her charred horn. "I just hope it still works." Then she gently touched her horn to Dracula's chest.

Luke cradled Dracula's head. Penny held her breath. Natalie crossed her fingers. Buttercup chewed a hole in Natalie's pocket.

But Dracula didn't move.

6

Tears welled in Penny's eyes and even Natalie had to wipe her cheeks. Buttercup gnawed on Natalie's shoestrings and looked away from Dracula's crumpled body.

"Your horn has lost its magic," Luke cried. "Poor, poor Dracula."

"No, it's working. Look," Kirin cried. "It just needed time."

Luke thought he saw Dracula's wings move. Then his link's eyes fluttered open. "Oh Dracula," Luke said, holding the dragon's head in his lap. "You're going to be okay."

Dracula staggered up from the ground with Luke's help. "Turkberries. Need turkberries," Dracula said.

Luke laughed through his tears. "No. No turkberries." Although truthfully, he would have given Dracula a whole boatful of turkberries, if he'd had them.

"You did it!" Penny hugged her link.

Kirin smiled. "Of course. I am a unicorn, after all."

"Well that's just great," Natalie said. "But we still don't know where we're going. So we're not any better off than before."

"Maybe we are," Penny said. She carefully unrolled the very old, very dirty piece of parchment that Louis had given her.

Luke leaned over her shoulder. "We can use Louis' map to guide us."

Natalie watched as Buttercup traced a claw along the river through an area called the Goblin Lands. "That's where the Queen lives. I'm sure it's where we'll find Leery."

Natalie groaned. "It looks like a long way."

Luke nodded. "We'd better get started."

Penny waved at Louis and shouted across the river, "Thanks, Louis!"

"Shhh," Luke told her. "We are in Goblin Land. We might want to keep quiet."

"Good advice," Kirin said, looking over her shoulder. "We should move quickly and quietly."

Penny led the way, consulting her map as she went. For a while, they scrambled over large boulders, but those quickly changed to massive trees, creating a dark tunnel for them to walk through. The longer they walked, the colder it became. Wind rattled branches and leaves whipped across the trail.

"This is totally creepy," Natalie said.

"Shhh," Luke said. "Do you want more goblin goo on your head?"

Natalie's hands flew to her hair and the three kids looked up in the treetops, but all they saw were branches shivering in the wind.

Natalie was quiet for a long time, until she whispered, "Look, aren't they pretty?"

Hundreds of tiny creatures encircled them. Their bodies glowed a soft green, and their wings made a tinkling sound. "Are they fireflies?" Luke asked.

"I think they're fairies," Penny said. The music of the fairies' wings filled the air. The kids swayed with the music and as the fairies moved, the kids followed them. Buttercup frantically pulled on Natalie's hand. "Mustn't go with them."

"Don't be silly," Natalie said. "They are so adorable. I want to catch one and keep it in a birdcage in my room."

Dracula knocked his head into Luke's butt. "Bad. Bad."

But Luke just patted his dragon, never looking away from the fairies that hovered in front of his face. "Don't worry. Everything's fine."

Kirin touched Penny with her horn. The horn's power was just enough to shake Penny away from the fairies' mesmerizing power. She saw the little creatures for what they really were, vicious fairies with fangs. "Pixies!" screeched Penny.

The pixies swarmed around Penny and snatched the map away. Before Kirin or Penny could react, the little creatures shredded the ancient parchment into dust. Then the pixies turned on the kids, snarling to show their fangs.

"You won't get us!" screamed Penny, throwing open her backpack and pulling out a bag of vinegar potato chips.

"This is no time for a snack," Natalie said, gasping as she used her backpack to knock away the dive-bombing pixies.

Penny smashed the bag between her hands and threw crumbs at the pixies. Whenever a crumb hit one, it disappeared in a tiny poof of black salt.

"Help me," Penny told Luke. The two of them tossed crumbs into the air.

Whack! A pixie disappeared.

Whack! Another one gone.

In only moments, the pixies had disappeared.

"We got them," Luke said in satisfaction.

"Not all of them," Natalie said, pointing to two glowing creatures disappearing through the woods.

"Me get!" Dracula said, flapping off into the dark woods.

"Dracula, come back here," Luke yelled. "I don't want anything to happen to you." He'd almost lost Dracula once; Luke couldn't stand to let it happen again.

"What were those?" Luke asked as Dracula landed safely beside him.

"Pixies," Penny explained, "and one way to battle them is with salt. Luckily I had those chips in case we met with Snuffles." Snuffles was the giant spider that had woven an invisibility web for their links, and she just happened to love vinegar potato chips.

Natalie looked at Penny. "How in the world did you know about salt?"

Penny shrugged. "It was in one of Mr. Leery's books."

"Let's not stand around chatting," Kirin interrupted. "I'm sure those pixies were spies for the Queen."

"There's just one problem," Luke said.

"Just one?" Natalie snapped. "Seems to me like there's a bunch of problems, starting with being attacked by insane fairies in the middle of nowhere."

"With no food or water," Penny muttered.

"The worst part is that we're in goblin

territory without a map," Buttercup pointed out.

"What are we going to do?" Penny asked.

Before the kids could figure out their next step, a low rumbling sound came from deep in the woods. "Now what?" Luke whispered.

7

"What is that noise?" Penny asked. She rubbed at the goose bumps popping out on her arms.

Ever since they had crossed the Snake River the temperature had been dropping. A cold wind rattled the branches overhead, snapping brown leaves off limbs. "It's probably just the wind. No wonder the trees are all dying," Natalie said. "It's too cold."

Buttercup clung to the top of Natalie's sneakers. "That is no natural wind," Buttercup said. "Can't you feel how the air itself is almost solid? It can mean only one thing. It's a precursor."

"A what?" Luke asked.

Buttercup pulled at her whiskers so hard one of them bent. "A warning of something bad to come. The air itself is fleeing from what follows it."

"Bad," Dracula said. "Bad. Bad."

"How bad can it be?" Natalie asked.

Another rumble punctuated her words. It was deep and raspy, like a car with no wheels being dragged across a highway. "Whatever that is, it's getting closer," Penny said.

"Something sounds familiar," Kirin said, trying to remember. Her skin twitched as if a thousand flies were doing the jitterbug on her back, and Dracula hiccupped.

Penny stopped suddenly. "We should go back. Maybe Louis will help us."

"Good idea," Luke said, but the kids didn't have a chance to take three steps. Something big crash-landed right in front of them and tumbled across the clearing in a blur of hooves and tail and horn.

Penny and Luke jumped back. Natalie hid behind them. Dracula hiccupped. Kirin was the only one who wasn't scared.

"Flash!" she cried.

A bronze unicorn splayed across the clearing, his sides heaving as he struggled to gulp air. He scrambled up to greet Kirin. When their horns met a silver halo glowed.

"Flash is my uncle," Kirin explained to the others. "And the fastest unicorn of our herd."

Flash didn't dispute her. "Where are the elves, niece?" he asked. "Bridger assured us they would accompany you."

"They're stuck," Dracula said. "Stuck! Stuck!"

"In a rooting trap," Kirin added.

Flash tossed his head and snorted. "The Queen's work, no doubt."

Kirin bowed before Flash. "But we are determined in our mission," she said. "Even without them."

Flash glanced at the Keyholders huddled behind Kirin. "You haven't much time. My mission has been successful. I know exactly where Leery is being kept."

"Well, it's about time someone gave us information we could use," Natalie said. "Where is he?"

"The Cave of the Winds," Flash said in a flat voice.

"*Nooooooooo!*" squeaked Buttercup. Her tiny body shivered in horror. "Anywhere but there!"

"Why?" Luke asked. "What's wrong with windy caves?"

Buttercup clung to Natalie's shoes and nibbled at her stockings.

"Tell them," Dracula said. "Tell them!"

"Yes, tell us," Natalie said, giving her foot a little shake to dislodge the gnawing rat. "Before you have my clothes in shreds."

Buttercup looked up at her link. "It doesn't matter. We must go in order to save Mr. Leery."

"And Mo," added Kirin.

"We haven't time for this chitchat," Flash said. "Sentinels are hot on my trail."

"I know I'm going to regret asking this," Penny said, "but what exactly are sentinels?"

"Creatures created by the Queen's magic to guard her domain," Flash told her.

That's when Kirin realized she knew exactly what the rumbling sound in the distance was—the hunting roar of sentinels.

"They're like guard dogs," Kirin added. "Only worse."

"Much worse," Dracula said. "Worse! Worse!"

"Hide here, niece. I'll lead the sentinels off on a wild goose chase," Flash said. "Leave as soon as they're gone. I won't be able to run from them forever. When the sentinels realize they've been duped, they'll be mad. And believe me, you don't ever want to face a mad sentinel."

"Be safe," Kirin told her uncle as his muscles coiled to resume his run.

"And you," Flash said. Their horns briefly touched once more before he leaped out of the clearing.

"Quick, climb those trees," Kirin said.

"What about you?" Penny asked, not wanting to be separated from her link.

"I can take care of Kirin," Luke said. He frantically dug in his backpack and pulled out the invisibility web the spider Snuffles had weaved for them. He threw it over Kirin. The web was tattered, and some of Kirin's glorious white hide peeked through. The kids hoped the sentinels would be in such a hurry to catch up with Flash that they wouldn't notice. Penny threw leaves on top of the web, just in case.

The kids, Dracula, and Buttercup had barely scrambled into the trees when four giant animals slinked into the clearing where the kids had stood only a moment before.

Dead leaves and twigs matted the animals' bellies and their tails were covered with rust-colored scales. Paws the size of dinner plates scratched at the dirt with long dirty claws. They had the ears of wolves, but their snouts were that of a boar. Two yellow tusks curled up over their top lips and came to a jagged point right in front of their orange eyes.

The sentinels sniffed the dirt in the small clearing. Penny almost screamed when one of the sentinels started for the place where Kirin

was hiding, but luckily another sentinel pointed its snout to the sky and roared from deep within its chest. It was the same rumbling sound the kids had been hearing. The other sentinels grunted and followed the leader as the beasts crashed through the forest after Flash.

"That was close," Penny said.

"Too close," Luke added.

Natalie didn't say a word. She was staring at the empty clearing. Penny snapped her fingers in front of Natalie's eyes. "Come on," Penny said. "We have to move it before they come back."

That was enough to send Natalie scrambling down the tree. "Which way do we go? Which way?" she muttered.

Buttercup scampered up to Natalie's shoulder and tugged on her hair. Hard. "That's what *you* have to figure out."

"Me?" Natalie shrieked. "Why me?"

"If only we had the troll's map. I bet it showed where those windy caves are," Luke said.

"They're called the Cave of the Winds," Buttercup said softly. "Not windy caves."

"What's the difference?" Penny asked.

Buttercup spat out the strand of Natalie's hair she had been nibbling. "The name is misleading. It's a magical place, one that was once used to benefit all of the Realm. But since the Queen's reign, it has become a vortex of violence where weather is held, mixed, and boiled until the Queen needs it to set loose upon her enemies. It will be dangerous for us. Very dangerous."

"Everything about the Shadow Realm is dangerous," Luke said.

"Only because the Queen rules over it," Kirin said. "But we can stop her."

"We *must* stop her," Buttercup added.

"How can we do that when we don't even know where the caves are?" Penny asked.

Natalie had been standing with her eyes closed. "I think I know where they are," she said. She sank to the ground, picked up a stick, and started scratching in the dirt. Buttercup held tight to her sleeve and watched.

"No," Buttercup said. "They're farther to the north. Remember?"

Natalie closed her eyes for a few moments, then nodded. "You're right, Buttercup. Help me."

Together, the two links murmured as Natalie continued scratching in the dirt. Finally finished, she looked up at Penny and Luke. "This is the way."

Buttercup gave a satisfied nod. "She's right."

"How did you figure that out?" Luke asked.

"I remembered Louis' map," Natalie said. "I closed my eyes and sort of redrew it in my mind. Buttercup helped."

Penny and Luke squatted in the dirt near Natalie's drawing.

"According to this, it isn't far from here," Luke said.

"No," Buttercup told him. "But don't be fooled. It will not be easy."

"Nothing ever is," Penny said, "with the Boggart Queen calling the shots."

8

It was farther than the kids thought. They walked for hours without speaking, afraid that more sentinels would be patrolling the perimeter of the Queen's domain. The sun remained hidden behind dense clouds, and as the day drew closer to evening the air grew thicker. Moss-covered ground gradually gave way to broken rock. Scraggly trees struggling to live rattled their branches as the trail climbed to meet a line of jagged cliffs.

Finally Natalie could take it no more. "I'm going to die of thirst," she muttered. "And no one will know what happened to me because you guys will be dead, too."

Penny rolled her eyes. She was exhausted and in no mood for Natalie's complaining. "We would have had some water if you hadn't washed your hair."

"Don't worry," Luke said. "I think we're almost there." He used Mr. Leery's walking stick to point through the mist that circled their ankles. The kids walked on until they reached the side of a cliff that soared straight up and became lost in heavy clouds.

"There's a trail," Penny said, pointing to a path that crisscrossed its way up the cliff.

In the distance the group heard strange noises. It sounded exactly like the cackles a witch makes in a scary movie. Luke used Mr. Leery's walking stick to struggle through vines and undergrowth—all of which snatched and grabbed at their ankles. The strange cackling grew louder, and it felt as if the branches themselves watched with spying eyes. Suddenly, a flurry of wings crashed through the air above them.

Natalie screamed and covered her hair. "Bats!"

The bats flew around the kids' heads before they veered off. "Those weren't normal bats," Luke told them.

"Of course not," Penny said. "They aimed right at us and fully intended to suck our blood. It was definitely no accident."

"The Queen sent them," Natalie agreed, wrapping her hair around her neck.

The fog was thicker and they could barely see each other. Luke grabbed Natalie's hand so they wouldn't lose each other. Normally Natalie wouldn't have held Luke's hand for a million dollars, but this time she held on tight.

"I have a bad feeling about this place," Penny said as she reached for Natalie's other hand. Kirin and Dracula hovered nearby, snuggling up against their links.

Buttercup scampered up Natalie's tights and dove into her pocket.

KA-BOOM!

A bolt of lightning lit up the sky and rain poured down on their heads. The wind gusted so hard, the kids had to lean into it just to keep from falling back.

"We're getting close to the cave," Buttercup shouted. Her tiny voice was whipped away. "Be prepared for anything."

The walking stick in Luke's hand pulled him to his knees. Dracula fluttered overhead, his wings battling the wind.

"Are you okay?" Penny asked Luke.

"I think his stick knows Mr. Leery is near," Luke answered. The walking stick continued to vibrate until it scratched at the face of the cliff wall.

KA-BOOM!

The closeness of the thunder caused the Keyholders to clutch at each other. Kirin leaned against Penny, and Dracula landed on Luke's left shoulder. Luke stooped under Dracula's weight, and Mr. Leery's walking staff touched against the cliff wall.

In that instant the rock wall before them shimmered to reveal an opening in the cliff face.

Dracula fluttered off Luke's shoulder, causing the walking stick to fall away from the wall. The cave entrance disappeared; the wall became solid again.

"Did you see it?" Penny shouted over the wind. "Did you see the cave?"

Luke and Natalie nodded. "But where did it go?" Natalie asked. The kids felt along the cliff wall, searching for a hole.

"It's a hidden entrance," Kirin said.

The walking stick seemed to know exactly where it was. "Follow me," Luke said as the stick pulled his arm.

The fog swirled about their legs, almost becoming solid. Penny reached out for Natalie and Luke again as she fought against the thick wall of white clouds. It was so thick, it caught in her throat.

"I . . . I . . . I can't breathe," Penny gasped as she gripped Luke's hand. "Don't let go of me, whatever you do."

From somewhere close they heard what sounded like voices. Cackling voices that spoke in a strange language.

The walking stick suddenly stuck to the cliff like a magnet.

"The opening is there," Natalie said. "I feel it."

"Where?" Luke asked. "I can't see anything!" Luke pounded the rock wall with Mr. Leery's walking stick. When the stick met stone, the cliff wall dissolved right in front of their eyes, leaving a gaping hole that led inside the mountain.

Buttercup held tight to Natalie as the kids stooped to enter the cave. Dracula and Kirin weren't far behind.

Buttercup jumped from Natalie's pocket and scurried across the small cave to a large boulder. The tiny rat frantically clawed at the rock.

"Stop that," Natalie said. "You're going to ruin your nail polish."

"I don't care about my nails," Buttercup said. "We have to free Leery."

"Free Mr. Leery?" Luke asked. "From where?"

Buttercup squealed. "He's inside the rock! Can't you feel it?"

Natalie looked at Buttercup before closing her eyes.

"This is no time for a nap," Luke told her.

"Shhh," Kirin warned. "Don't you see?

Natalie has the sense. She can *feel* things. Let her do her work."

The kids stared at Natalie as she stood, slightly swaying, in the damp cave. When her eyes opened, it looked like Natalie had seen a ghost. "He *is* here," she said, placing her hand on the boulder.

Luke and Penny stared at the giant rock. "Nobody can survive being trapped in stone," Penny whispered.

"Which is why we must hurry," Kirin said. "Before Mr. Leery and Mo are forever turned to rock."

"Quick, hold hands," Luke said.

"What good will that do?" Natalie said.

"Didn't you notice?" Luke asked. "When we were all connected we were able to see into the cave. Maybe now we can see inside the rock."

The three kids held hands. Dracula pushed between Luke and Penny. Kirin stood between Natalie and Penny. Buttercup clung to Natalie's shoelaces. They had a clear vision of Mr. Leery lying on the other side of the boulder. He wasn't moving.

"He's here!" Penny shouted. They all pushed against the boulder until their faces dripped sweat, but the giant rock wouldn't budge.

Penny stepped back to get her breath and stumbled over Mr. Leery's walking stick.

"The stick!" Penny said. "It helped us find the entrance. Maybe it can help us move the boulder." She snatched the stick off the ground and banged it against the boulder.

Nothing happened.

"Let me try," Natalie said. "After all, I'm the one with the advanced powers." She grabbed it, knocking it against the rock.

Nothing.

"It has to work," Penny cried. "What are we doing wrong?"

Luke held up Mr. Leery's walking stick. "Maybe the power is too much for one of us. We have to work together to use it."

"You're right!" Penny said, remembering that she was clutching Luke's hand when he used the staff the first time.

Luke held the walking stick in front of him. Penny and Natalie grabbed it with both

their hands. Just as the three friends pointed it toward the boulder, Kirin touched the stick with her horn, Buttercup leaped on one end and Dracula hiccupped a flame that caused the other end to glow.

The mountain shook with a ferocious force at the touch of the walking stick. Jagged shards of rock fell from above them and crashed to the floor. Stone ground against stone as the boulder rolled away from the wall.

And there, before them, a very pale Mr. Leery lay on a shelf of stone. He was still. Very still, just like the rock.

"I've got you, now. I've got you all," a voice like fingernails tearing through aluminum foil cackled from behind them. "The Queen will be so happy. At last I shall be rewarded! At last!"

The kids turned, peering through a cloud of dust and falling rock.

Luke's scream caught in his throat. Penny forgot to breathe. Natalie nearly fainted. For there, blocking the entrance of the cave, was a being so ugly it would give them nightmares until they were a hundred and two.

Squeak! A horrible grating noise filled the air as a gigantic cage slammed down around the kids, Mr. Leery, and the kids' links.

They were trapped!

9

Natalie threw herself against the bars of the cage, trying to squeeze through. "Ouch!" She fell back. "There's some kind of spell, keeping us in. It zapped me."

Buttercup nodded and kept hidden in Natalie's pocket. "A container spell formed with enchanted glass. No way in or out until the harpy leaves."

"Is that what that horrible thing is?" Luke whispered. The three kids looked at the cackling creature. It had the face of a two-thousand-year-old woman, the wings and body of a rotting vulture, and jagged claws that snaked out from her hands like daggers.

"It stinks like last year's gym socks," Natalie said, holding her nose. "If we don't get out of here soon, I'm going to throw up."

"Maybe Leery can help us," Kirin suggested. The kids bent over Mr. Leery. He was alive, but they couldn't get him to wake up, even when Natalie smacked his face.

"Let me try," Kirin said, lowering her horn.

Buttercup shook her head. "No, this is the same spell that was cast on Mo. Your magic will be of no help here."

"What are we going to do?" Natalie said.

"Mr. Leery was nothing but bait," Penny whispered.

"And we walked right into the trap," Luke said. "A trap set just for us."

"Why in the world did Mr. Leery choose us to be Keyholders anyway? I can't do anything right," Penny said, big puddles of tears standing in her dark brown eyes.

"The Queen is coming! The Queen is coming!" The harpy danced an evil jig and sang, ignoring the children's whispers. The kids huddled on the floor of the cave with their

links, close to Mr. Leery and as far away from the hideous harpy as they could get.

Luke put his hand on Penny's shoulder. "We'd still be battling pixies if it weren't for you."

Penny shook her head. "Anyone could find that in a book."

"But not everyone would know to look," Natalie said, surprising everyone. "Or take the time."

"If it wasn't for Luke and his perfect aim, we'd still be on the far side of the river," Penny said.

"And we'd be lost if it hadn't been for Natalie's ability to sense things," Luke added.

Natalie nodded. "It took all of us to make it this far."

"It doesn't matter now," Penny said, feeling defeated. "We're doomed."

The harpy laughed, sending chills down the kids' backs. "The Queen is on her way, riding her red dragon."

Now Dracula shivered. "Red dragons bad. Bad! Bad! Bad!"

"Wait a minute," Penny said, feeling hopeful again. "What did you say?"

Dracula flapped his wings. "Bad dragon."

"No," Penny said, pointing to Natalie.

Natalie rolled her eyes. "What are you talking about? I'm about to get crispy fried by an evil harpy who's got me in a cage. I can't remember everything I said about you reading books."

"That's it!" Penny yelled. She ripped open her backpack and pulled out a thick book.

"You carried that heavy thing all this way?" Natalie said. "You're crazier than I thought."

"It's from Mr. Leery's library. I thought we might need it." Penny zipped through the index until she found what she was looking for, then flipped pages backward and started reading.

"Um, Penny. I don't think this is the time for a story," Luke said, tapping her shoulder. "We should be doing something."

Penny looked up from the book and smiled. "You're exactly right. It says here in this book that the only thing that frightens harpies away is the sound of a brass instrument."

"Well, that would be great if we had a trombone handy," Luke said, "but I'm fresh out."

"But Natalie's not," Penny said.

"What?" Natalie said with a puzzled look on her face. And then in a moment of recognition Natalie smiled, too. She pulled two MP3 players out of her bag and turned the first one on full blast with the mini speakers attached.

Nothing happened. "Don't you ever check your batteries?" Luke groaned.

Natalie gave him a dirty look, plugged the speakers into the other one, and turned it on. Loud music blared.

"It has to have sounds from brass instruments," Penny yelled. "Trumpets. Trombones. Tubas."

Natalie twirled the dial until trumpets blasted out of the tiny player. The harpy stopped singing and flew away crying, *"No! No! Nooooooo!!!!"* The kids heard her screeching the whole way.

"Try the cage now," Buttercup said. "When the harpy left, her spell may have weakened."

"Stand back," Kirin said. She gave a massive kick to the door with her back legs. The glass shattered and the door clattered to the ground.

"Hurry," Penny said, giving Kirin a quick hug. "Let's get Mr. Leery out of here before the Queen comes."

10

They weren't fast enough.

The Queen, astride her red dragon, arrived at the mouth of the cave. The kids froze and stared at the beautiful woman before them. Her long blond hair flowed over a gown of shining white silk, and a sparkling crown of diamonds and emeralds sat atop her head. Even her face glowed with radiance.

"She's the prettiest person in the whole world," Natalie said, taking a step toward her.

Luke grabbed Natalie and pulled her back. "She's a boggart. Remember, she can look however she wants. Remember what *real* boggarts looked like?"

Penny shivered as she thought back to the boggart spy named Bobby who had infiltrated their school. He had been able to change shapes. At first he looked like a boy. A strange boy, but still a boy. When he'd changed into his boggart form, the kids caught a glimpse of what real boggarts look like. It wasn't a pretty sight.

Natalie couldn't take her eyes off the Queen, while Dracula stared at the red dragon. It was easily five times bigger than Dracula. Luke noticed right away that the red dragon didn't have wings.

"Welcome to my kingdom," the Queen said in a sweet voice that sounded like a finely tuned piano.

The Keyholders backed up. Buttercup squealed and dove deeper into Natalie's pocket.

"I'm not going down without a fight," Penny said.

"There's no need for anyone to fight," the Queen said, waving her staff. Immediately the music in Natalie's MP3 player stopped.

Natalie stared, transfixed by the Queen's

beauty. "No need to fight," Natalie muttered.

"Oh yes, there is," Penny screamed. "You've hurt Mr. Leery and Mo. Put them back the way they're supposed to be."

"Um, Penny," Luke whispered. "Maybe we shouldn't make her mad."

The red dragon lay down so the Queen could step lightly off his back. She glided toward the children.

"Don't come any closer," Penny warned.

The Queen laughed. "Or what? What can three pitiful children do against the Boggart Queen? What was that stupid Leery thinking? Making infants into Keyholders? It will be so easy to defeat you. Then the world will be mine. The *whole* world. Now, how about I get rid of this troublesome bookworm first?"

The Queen aimed her staff at Penny. Luke threw the first thing that he could grab . . . Mr. Leery's walking stick. It smacked into the Queen's staff. Her staff exploded in a burst of blue sparks. The red dragon reared up in panic, snorting flames all around the cave.

Kirin jumped in front of the kids and Mr. Leery, shielding them with her body.

The Boggart Queen was not so lucky. Her silk gown turned black and sooty. Her beauty was gone, replaced by her true self. The Queen was now an ape-like creature with enormous pointed ears and glowing yellow eyes. She groveled on the floor, pawing at the ashes of her staff. "What have you done?" she cried. "What have you done?"

Dracula didn't waste any time. He flew right into the huge dragon's face and roared. The red dragon was taken by surprise and toppled backward, falling out of the cave and down the cliff.

The Queen screeched and ran to the mouth of the cave. "My dragon!"

Luke scrambled to pick up Mr. Leery's staff. When the Queen turned back around, Kirin was waiting for her. With one toss of her head, Kirin pushed the Queen inside the cage.

Together, Penny, Luke, and Buttercup shoved the cage until the broken door was blocked by the solid rock of the cave wall.

The Queen rattled the bars. She jumped up and down. But the cage was too strong. "You can't run from me!" The Queen shook her fist at them.

"Oh, yes we can," Natalie said, no longer hypnotized by the Queen's beauty. "You're just a mean ugly boggart!"

"Hurry," Buttercup shrieked, "before she breaks the enchanted glass."

The kids scrambled down the rocks as quickly as they could into the driving rain. Luke and Penny dragged a limp Mr. Leery between them. Mr. Leery regained consciousness only long enough to whisper, "Well done, Keyholders."

Luke panted. "We'll never be fast enough to escape all the creatures she'll send after us."

Natalie felt like giving up, but she stumbled and grabbed onto Leery's staff. A misty vision flashed before her eyes and suddenly she knew how to get home, stopping only long enough to save the elves along the way.

"Kirin, I know you're not a pack horse, but

could you and Dracula help us get back to the border?" Natalie asked. "Please?"

Kirin looked at Natalie in surprise. Usually Natalie didn't ask. She told. But this time she'd even said please. Kirin nodded and then she opened her mouth to make a sound, but nothing came out. At least nothing the kids could hear.

Kirin's call worked because in seconds a bronze unicorn stood before them. "Flash, at your service."

Flash kneeled down and Natalie climbed aboard with Buttercup in her pocket. Penny held Mr. Leery on Kirin and Luke got the surprise of his life when Dracula tossed him on his back. Then they were racing through the forest. Dracula and Luke actually flew, while Flash and Kirin ran as only unicorns can.

Epilogue

"I may have lost this battle," the Boggart Queen screeched after them. "But I am not defeated. I AM NOT DEFEATED!"

Her scream shattered the enchanted glass and made boulders tumble from the cliffs as the Keyholders and their friends fled down the path.

The Queen's knuckles pounded the cliff. Her claws dug deep crevices in the rock. Slobber spewed across the cave and splattered the broken cage. Where it landed, the bars sizzled.

"I will get them," the Boggart Queen growled. "If it's the last thing I do. I. Will. Get. THEM!!!"

Goblins, boggarts, and hobgoblins cowered in the trees as their queen threw her tantrum.

One lone boggart clutching something pink against his chest crept from his hiding place and approached the angry queen. "If it pleases your majesty," he said.

"Nothing will please your majesty," she seethed, "until I have those Keyholders in my clutches. NOTHING!"

The boggart blinked and took a step back, but then he continued forward, one tentative step at a time. "Perhaps this will help?" he said with a voice full of question and hope.

The Queen turned her yellow eyes on the boggart. "I know you," she said.

The outline of the boggart's body began to blur and turn hazy as he shape-shifted into what looked like a very strange boy.

"Ah, yes," the Queen said. "Bobby was the name we gave you for your last mission, wasn't it?"

The boggart nodded his human-shaped head. "It was an honor to serve my Queen.

Now I offer you this," he said. He tentatively held out the pink object and waited for the Queen to snatch it from his trembling hands. "It's the humdrum's notebook," he told her. "The one they call Natalie."

The Queen of Boggarts bent back the cover, not worrying about the jagged crease she created. As she flipped through the pages, the Queen's look of fury turned into a grin.

And so it was that the Queen of Boggarts hatched her new plan.

Turn the page for a sneak peek at

KEYHOLDERS #4

THE WRONG SIDE OF MAGIC

1

Snap!

The troll's yellow fangs barely missed Luke.

Whack!

Luke slammed his basketball into the belly of the troll. The hideously ugly creature stumbled backward toward the bushes and trees behind Luke's house. It lashed out at Luke, but Penny was too fast. She bent over behind the monster and tripped it.

Long stringy hair and huge treelike arms flew backward. When the troll hit the ground, the whole backyard shook.

"Get out of the way," Luke's neighbor, Natalie, yelled. She stormed past him with an enormous high-beam flashlight. The light cut through the evening darkness, putting the troll in the spotlight.

The troll let out a deafening roar, covered its face with its long barklike fingers, and crashed through the trees. "Hurry!" Penny said. "Fix the border."

"Links, come quick!" Luke yelled.

Three creatures bounced into the yard.

A dazzling white unicorn landed beside Penny, a small green and silver dragon beside Luke, and a rat scrambled onto Natalie's toe. For a few moments, none of them spoke. All six of them concentrated on the row of bushes and trees.

A wave of energy vibrated in the air. Immediately, the trees broken by the troll were made whole again. It was as if the troll had never invaded Luke's backyard. But the kids knew differently, and so did their magical links.

Natalie quickly switched off the flashlight to keep the magical creatures from being seen by anyone in Luke's house.

Penny's unicorn, Kirin, spoke first, "What's going on? That's the third break in the border this week. The border is getting as holey as Mr. Leery's underwear."

Dracula, Luke's dragon, bounced up and down. "Break. Break. Break." Luke's dragon was a dragon of few words, but a lot of energy.

Luke patted his dragon and said, "Kirin is right. Something strange is going on. Don't you feel it?"

Penny shivered. Strange was exactly how she'd felt ever since they'd found out that the old man who lived next to Luke was a mysterious Keyholder who kept the magical world from leaking into the real world. She had known him all her life as Mr. Leery, a nice old man who gave her birthday presents and liked to putter around his yard with his cat Mo.

But nothing was as it seemed. Mo wasn't a cat at all: He was really a shape-shifting griffin. He was also a link—an animal from the magical realm that had formed an unbreakable lifelong bond with Mr. Leery. Just like

Dracula the dragon was Luke's link and Kirin was her own.

Being linked to a unicorn was the best thing that had ever happened to Penny. At first, Natalie had been bummed to have a rat as a link, but now they were great buddies. Although Penny had to admit that having a rat for a link wasn't nearly as wonderful as a unicorn.

The whole thing made Penny's head spin if she thought about it too much, especially the part where Mr. Leery had chosen the three of them to be the new Keyholders.

"I do feel something strange going on," Natalie said. "I don't know what it is but I don't like it."

"Wait just a minute," Penny said. "How did you know to use that big flashlight on the troll?" Usually Penny was the one who figured out how to deal with the bad creatures that sometimes slipped through the border.

Natalie giggled. "I used my new phone with its wireless Internet connection."

Luke groaned. Natalie had every known gadget available. She was the most spoiled kid he knew.

"When I saw that troll thing out my window," Natalie continued, "I typed 'trolls' in my phone and it said that they didn't like bright lights."

"Genius!" Natalie's link said. Buttercup beamed obvious pride.

"If I'm such a genius, then why haven't I had my installation ceremony?" Natalie snapped.

"Not that again." Luke grabbed his basketball off the ground and walked away from Natalie. She was always complaining about something.

"Mr. Leery promised as soon as he was feeling better he would officially make you a Keyholder," Penny said, edging away from Natalie.

"He's taking too long," Natalie complained. "I think he's just pretending to be sick so we have to do all the border work ourselves."

Being a Keyholder wasn't as glamorous as the kids had thought it would be. Mostly, it meant trying to sense where the border was weak so bad magical creatures from the other side couldn't sneak through. When that happened, they had to mend the break in the border. They didn't even want to think about the chaos that would erupt if bad magic was set loose in the real world.

"You know that's not true!" Penny said. "Mr. Leery really is sick."

Kirin nudged Penny on the shoulder with her horn. "Maybe he picked up some germ when the Boggart Queen trapped him in that rock," the unicorn said.

Natalie's cheeks paled. She didn't like to think about when the Boggart Queen kidnapped Mr. Leery and used him as bait to trap the three kids. It had only been by chance that the three kids and their links had figured out how to break Mr. Leery free from the spell that kept him sealed inside solid rock.

"Germs!" Dracula sputtered as he jumped up and down in front of Luke. "Ick! Ick! Ick!"

Luke reached out and put his hand on Dracula's head to stop him from bouncing.

"Mr. Leery seems to be getting better," Luke told Natalie. "It won't be too much longer before he has your installation ceremony."

Buttercup put a paw on Natalie's leg. "Don't worry, I'm sure you'll have your ceremony soon."

Natalie stomped her foot and sent Buttercup skittering away. "It's not fair," she told Luke and Penny. "You've had your ceremony. I want mine."

"Big deal," Luke said, bouncing the ball. "You have everything else." Natalie lived in the biggest house in Morgantown, complete with a home theater and swimming pool.

"Come on," Penny said, "let's finish checking the border so we can go home and work on our science projects." Although Natalie wasn't her favorite person, Penny could understand Natalie wanting the ceremony. It had been the most amazing event of Penny's life. She had received the blessings of fairies, elves, centaurs, and even a genie. It made her smile just to think about the beauty and mystery of it all.

Natalie turned her back on Penny and Luke. "No. I'm going home now. I've had it with stinky trolls and borders."

"You can't," Penny said. "What if there's been another breach in the border?"

Luke threw the basketball and it swished through the net. "Natalie's right. There's never been more than one break in the border in a day. I'm sure everything is fine. Let's just get our homework done. My mom will ground me if I have another late assignment."

The three kids were all in the same fifth grade class, and since finding out they were Keyholders, their grades had slipped. After all, it was hard keeping their minds on math and social studies when they were the only kids in Morgantown who knew an evil Boggart Queen was trying to take over the world.

Penny looked at the thick hedge of trees and bushes. The trees, bushes, vines, and weeds were so thick they made a living wall. She still felt that funny feeling, but maybe she was being silly. After all, Natalie and

Luke were much better at being Keyholders. She had trouble finding weak spots in the border and they were both becoming experts. And she really did need to work on her science project. She hadn't even chosen her topic yet.

"All right," Penny said with a sigh. "But don't forget to wear your silver bracelets just in case."

Luke rolled his eyes. "Yes, mother," he teased.

Mr. Leery had given them each a special silver bracelet to protect them from goblins and boggarts, but Luke thought they were girly. Still, he wore the bracelet tucked under his shirtsleeve—just in case.

Luke and Penny hugged their links goodbye and watched as they slipped back into the total darkness of Mr. Leery's yard next door. One of the best parts about being a Keyholder was the lifelong bond they had with their links. One of the hardest parts was being separated from them. But their links needed to stay hidden from everyone, and the only safe place for hiding was in Mr. Leery's yard. Thanks to the new magic the old wizard had learned for surrounding his yard with a muffling spell, no one on the outside would notice an energetic dragon and a bored unicorn hanging out in the yard at the end of Rim Drive. It was much safer than hiding them under an invisibility web.

Natalie scooped up her link and went across the street to her house without even a backward glance. Buttercup, the rat, was definitely a lot easier to hide than a unicorn or a dragon.

Penny and Luke watched Natalie until she had closed the door to her huge house.

Luke sighed and headed inside his house to search the Internet for a possible science project until he couldn't keep his eyes open.

In her room, Penny looked through library book after library book for the perfect science project. Finally, she fell asleep with a book in her lap.

Natalie, on the other hand, took a relaxing bubble bath, painted her fingernails pink and

Buttercup's claws purple, and fell asleep listening to her MP3 player.

Everything seemed calm on the last street of Morgantown, but in the early hours of the morning, Buttercup jumped on Natalie's head.

"Hurry!" Buttercup screeched. "Wake up!"

Natalie rolled over, sending Buttercup flying across the room.

"Leave me alone," Natalie grumbled. "It's still dark outside."

Buttercup scrambled up the pink bedspread and pinched Natalie. "You must get up. It's an emergency."

Natalie sat straight up in her bed, sending Buttercup head over heels to the bottom of the bed.

"Oh no, there's been another breech!" Natalie screamed.

ABOUT THE AUTHORS

MARCIA THORNTON JONES enjoys reading more than anything else. As a teacher, her favorite part of the school day was sharing books with her students. It was that love of reading that drew her to writing. She wanted to write the same kinds of stories that she and her students enjoyed reading. One afternoon she mentioned to the school librarian that she'd always had an interest in writing. The librarian, Debbie Dadey, shared a desire to write stories that would encourage reading skills while promoting a true joy of reading. The next afternoon, Marcia and Debbie met while their students were at lunch and began writing. That story, "Vampires Don't Wear Polka Dots," became the first book in their bestselling series, The Adventures of the Bailey School Kids.

Marcia lives in Lexington, Kentucky, with her husband, Stephen, and their two cats. For more information about Marcia, her books, author visits, and for activities related to her books, check out Marcia's Web site: **www. marciatjones.com.**

Debbie Dadey taught first grade before becoming a librarian. It was while teaching that she realized how much she wanted to write a book for reluctant readers. Her first book, coauthored with fellow teacher Marcia Thornton Jones, was about a mysterious teacher. Since then, Debbie and Marcia have collaborated on more than 125 books with sales of over forty million copies.

Debbie lives in Bucks County, Pennsylvania, with her husband, three dogs, and three children. Visit **www.debbiedadey.com** for Keyholder games, character cards, and fun activities.

Starscape

Award-Winning
Science Fiction and Fantasy
for Ages 10 and up

STARSCAPE

www.tor-forge.com/starscape